WHAT IS IT?™

WHAT IS IT?™

Written by
NICOLE HOANG

Illustrated by
DUSTIN NGUYEN

Designers
**Scott Newman
& Kelsey Dieterich**

Editor
Sierra Hahn

ROSS RICHIE CEO & Founder
MATT GAGNON Editor-in-Chief
FILIP SABLIK President of Publishing & Marketing
STEPHEN CHRISTY President of Development
LANCE KREITER VP of Licensing & Merchandising
PHIL BARBARO VP of Finance
BRYCE CARLSON Managing Editor
MEL CAYLO Marketing Manager
SCOTT NEWMAN Production Design Manager
IRENE BRADISH Operations Manager
CHRISTINE DINH Brand Communications Manager
SIERRA HAHN Senior Editor
DAFNA PLEBAN Editor
SHANNON WATTERS Editor
ERIC HARBURN Editor
WHITNEY LEOPARD Associate Editor
JASMINE AMIRI Associate Editor
CHRIS ROSA Associate Editor
ALEX GALER Assistant Editor
CAMERON CHITTOCK Assistant Editor
MARY GUMPORT Assistant Editor
MATTHEW LEVINE Assistant Editor
KELSEY DIETERICH Production Designer
JILLIAN CRAB Production Designer
MICHELLE ANKLEY Production Design Assistant
GRACE PARK Production Design Assistant
AARON FERRARA Operations Coordinator
ELIZABETH LOUGHRIDGE Accounting Coordinator
JOSÉ MEZA Sales Assistant
JAMES ARRIOLA Mailroom Assistant
HOLLY AITCHISON Operations Assistant
STEPHANIE HOCUTT Marketing Assistant
SAM KUSEK Direct Market Representative

(kaboom!)™

5670 Wilshire Boulevard, Suite 450, Los Angeles, CA 90036-5679. Printed in China. First Printing.

ISBN: 978-1-60886-835-3, eISBN: 978-1-61398-506-9

This book is dedicated to
both our kids and their
spirit of sharing all they
create with us.

It's rather strange, I'd have to say,
I saw the thing just yesterday.

What is it?

What could it be?

Someone please answer this for me!

It was quite big with a little tail.
And huge ears that looked like shells.

The thing growled and went BOW-WOW.
And had a strange face that looked like a cow.

It nearly scared me half to death
with its smelly bad breath.

Without thinking, I ran away.
But the thing wanted me to stay.

It bit me once on the behind,
which made me realize it was not kind!

Scared, I looked down at the dirty, old ground.

And saw its big, giant feet...
and claws ready to tear out my meat!

Suddenly, it reached for my pocket,
which inside was my precious locket.

The thing took it and threw it to the ground!
And stomped on the locket 'til it turned brown.

As I watched in horror, my face turned red, and, finally, I socked it hard in the head.

Surprised, the thing looked at me.
I ran away and climbed up a tree.

And found out the thing can climb trees, too!
Like a monkey who escaped from a zoo!

Scared, I jumped back down
and landed hard on the ground.

I got up and ran down the road.
The thing hopped after me like a giant toad.

I ran faster and jumped into a lake.
The water was cold and I began to shake.

I turned around and could see the thing was scared, scared to wet its long, thick hair.

I laughed so hard, tears came to my eyes!
The thing stared at me, ready to die!

Suddenly, the thing ran away.
So fast, it didn't have time to say...

What it was or what's its name,
or why it even, ever came.

SPECIAL THANKS

Nicole would like to thank her mom and dad for showing her that anything is possible with a little hard work; her brothers and sisters for continuing their childhood conversations, including the one about what their next great invention should be; and her children for pretending to laugh at all her jokes and always being willing to do the running man dance with her. And finally, her husband, for always being supportive and letting her sleep in late on the weekends.

Dustin would like to thank his family and especially his mom for always supporting his career in illustration.

Special thanks to Sierra Hahn and Bryce Carlson for believing in this book and for pushing to a wider audience what was originally only meant as a simple story shared with our close ones on our wedding day.

Art by Nicole Hoang, Age 10